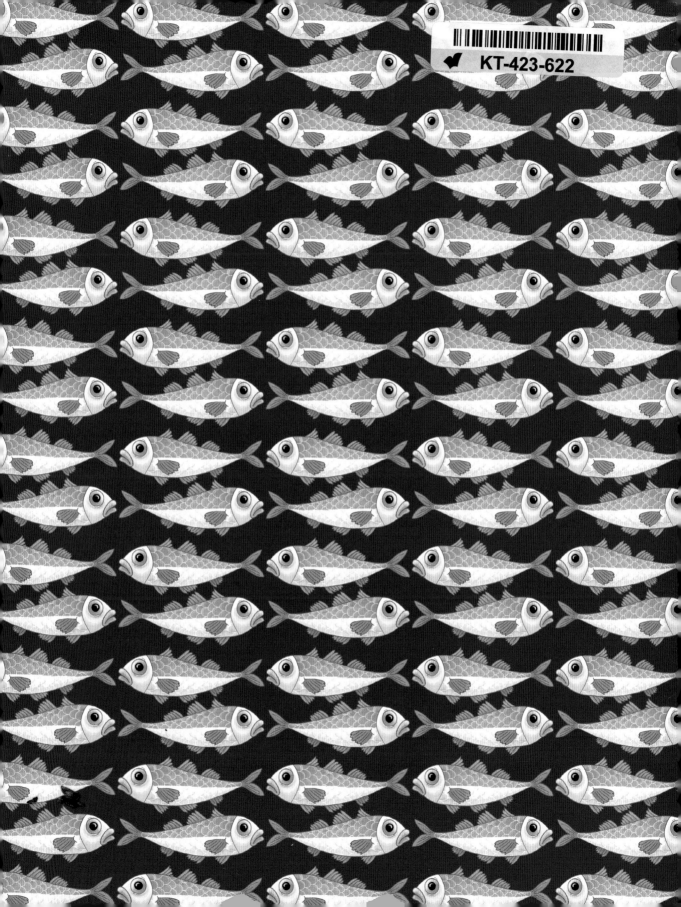

To Mum
P.B.

For my family and George
J.F.

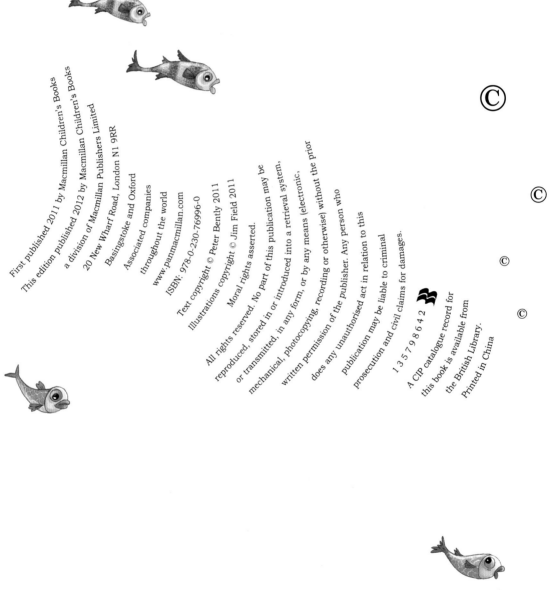

First published 2011 by Macmillan Children's Books

This edition published 2012 by Macmillan Children's Books

a division of Macmillan Publishers Limited

20 New Wharf Road, London N1 9RR

Basingstoke and Oxford

Associated companies

throughout the world

www.panmacmillan.com

ISBN: 978-0-230-76996-0

Text copyright © Peter Bently 2011

Illustrations copyright © Jim Field 2011

Moral rights asserted.

1 3 5 7 9 8 6 4 2

A CIP catalogue record for
this book is available from
the British Library.

Printed in China

PETER BENTLY · JIM FIELD

CATS AHOY!

MACMILLAN
CHILDREN'S BOOKS

One night by the harbour, the church bell struck ten
When Alfonso the cat overheard two old men:

"Did you hear?" said the first. "There's a boat on the way
Which will be in the harbour at first light of day.
It's laden with haddock from rudder to bow –
It's the biggest catch ever."
Alfonso thought . . .

WOW!

NO SCALLOPS
LEFT ON
THIS BOAT
OVERNIGHT

Off shot Alfonso as swift
as an arrow

Through alleys and gardens and
streets dark and narrow.

He told every cat to
prepare for a treat:
"Follow me and you'll get all
the fish you can eat!"

"There's a ship standing empty,
a three-masted clipper.
Meet there at midnight.
Her name is *The Kipper*."

A little while later, two terrified dogs
Turned tail at the sight of a great gang of mogs
Boarding *The Kipper* on soft silent paws
With pistols and cutlasses clamped in their jaws.

And then, while the townsfolk were tucked up and snoring,
The Kipper weighed anchor and slipped from its mooring
And steered a straight course for the deep ocean blue
With Captain Alfonso and all of his crew.

The trawler-boat skipper, Trelawney P. Craddock,
Looked down with delight on his huge haul of haddock.
"The biggest catch ever!" he thought with a smirk.
"I'll be famous and wealthy and won't need to work!"

But then . . . what was that? Craddock peered through the mist.
There was something close by — and that something just hissed.
He listened again, and there came a strange howling,
A grim ghoulish groaning, a terrible yowling . . .

"What's up?" gasped the mate. "No idea!" yelled the skipper.
Then . . . SHIP AHOY! From the mist sailed *The Kipper*.

And as she came close in the moon's eerie light
The fishermen shivered and trembled in fright.
For, as hard as they stared, not a soul could they see
– that bloodcurdling din! What on earth could it be?

"GREAT CODFISH!"

yelled Craddock with quivering lip,
"We're bein' attacked by . . .

In a panic the fishermen fled up the deck,
Leapt into the lifeboat, and paddled like heck.

(The cook, who had sneaked
down below for a snooze,
Was forced to abandon
his trousers and shoes.)

And once Craddock's crew had rowed too far to hear,
The voice of Alfonso cried,

"OK! All clear!"

One by one, furry faces popped
up with great glee,

"HEY, CHECK OUT
THAT HADDOCK!"

"FISHTASTIC!"

"YOWEE!"

"And now," said Alfonso,
"To Smugglers' Bay
For a great fishy feast!"
and the cats cried,

"HOORAY!"

In a small sheltered cove out of sight of the land
The sea-mogs scoffed haddock and danced on the sand.
As the bright rays of dawn were beginning to gleam
They sang,

"Yo-Ho-Ho
and a Carton of Cream!"

A day or two later, Trelawney P. Craddock
Was telling of phantoms who'd stolen his haddock.
"Their flag was two fishbones, I'm quite sure of that,
With something that looked like the skull of a . . . cat."

"A cat?" said the townsfolk. "A cat? Don't be daft!
Who's heard of cat-pirates?" and everyone laughed.
Yet something had happened that was rather weird.
Where were the cats? They had all disappeared!

They were gone for a week — a whole week without dinner,
But when they came back they were fatter, not thinner.
Some townsfolk began to add up two and two.
And questioned their cats, "Were you there?" "Was it you?"

But the cats had all taken a most solemn vow
Just to look up all sweetly and answer,

And whatever their crimes, the folk find to this day
When they question their moggies, that's all they will say.

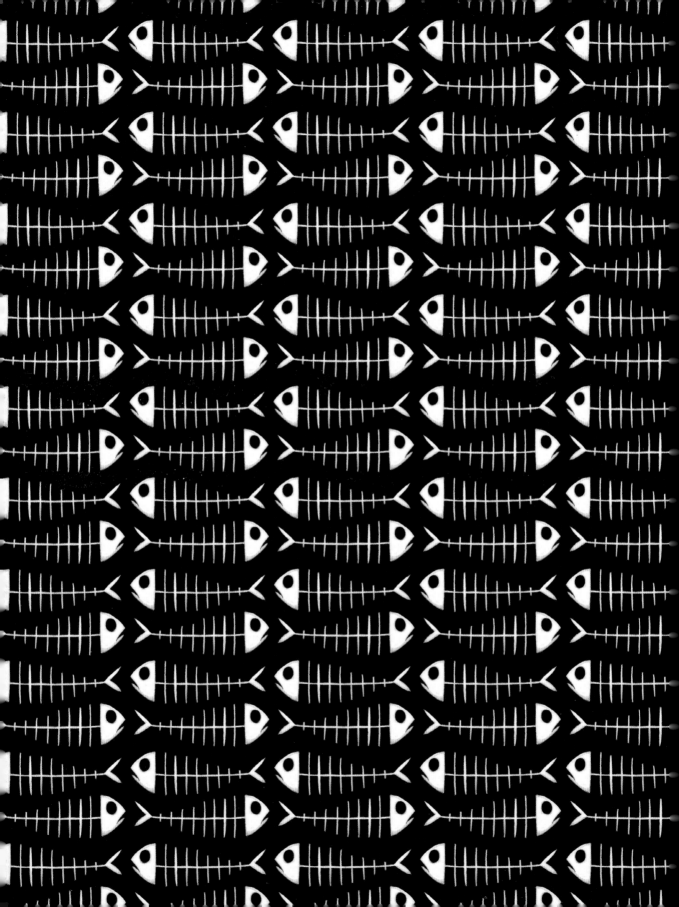